The Blue World:
Anunnaki Advent
(c) 2020
by
Paul Clayton

The Blue World: Anunnaki Advent

Paul Clayton

Published by Paul Clayton, 2024.

THE BLUE WORLD: ANUNNAKI ADVENT

First edition. January 1, 2024.

Copyright © 2024 Paul Clayton.

ISBN: 979-8224830527

Written by Paul Clayton.

Table of Contents

The book is dedicated to Zecharia Sitchin, author of the
Earth Chronicles series.

"And it came to pass, when people began to multiply on the face of the earth, and daughters were born unto them, the sons of God saw that they were fair; and they took wives for themselves of all that they chose..."
Genesis 6:2

ONE

The star-splattered blackness of space seen through the viewscreens normally filled Enki with awe, but now it seemed chaotic and foreboding. He sat alone on the bridge of the Mother Ship as it sped toward the Blue World. It was a mining planet and the most distant outpost of the Anunnaki, an ebony reptilian race, the most powerful race in the universe. Upon arrival, they would descend and Enki, first-born of their king, Anu the Great, would take over as Commander-of-Operations, an assignment he had not wanted. Enlil, his half-brother, would be his second-in-command. Although Enki was first-born, he was born of Anu's consort, while Enlil, second-born, was born of Anu's wife. This contributed to the never-ending competition between them for title, favor, and their father's love and respect. The forty-eight other Anunnaki going to the Blue World were the first cloned set sired by Anu, and his pride and joy.

Enki recalled a report on the Blue World he had once viewed with other Anunnaki. "A beautiful gem," one of his brothers had said afterward, "our treasure trove. Perhaps we shall go there one day."

"Perhaps," Enki had said at the time. But, he had thought, hopefully never, for he had heard enough stories of the Blue World to dissuade him—stories of the cold at the poles, the fetid jungles at the equator, and the violent storms.

After Enki's sixty years on Sithera, his last command, he had wanted to return to his home planet of Nibiru. But he had been ordered to relieve the Commander on the Blue World and take over the supervision of the mines and the gardens of Eden.

Enki was surprised that his father had chosen him. Perhaps it was Enki's training as a biologist that had led Anu to put him in command. It was imperative that the gardens flourish and produce so the Anunnaki would remain healthy enough to work the mines. Enki frowned. He had been honored, but he knew the appointment would further acerbate his uneasy relationship with his brother, Enlil.

Enki felt the ship begin its deceleration. His brothers began entering the bridge and taking their seats. Along with them, he watched the tiny spark that was the Blue World grow and grow until it filled the viewscreens. Enki and the others stared at the frozen rocky barrens of the planet's southern axis slowly scrolling by on the screens. After they'd seen the entire orb, Enki took his six lieutenants into the boardroom. Once more he went over the details of their assignment and the protocols that Anu and the Supreme Council of the Anunnaki had established for those who served on the Blue World.

Enki and his lieutenants, engineers, technicians, priests, and military officials would live at the temple complex above Eden and at the camp compound at Shuruppak. They would take over the operation of the gardens and the mines. They were not to interfere with the many lifeforms there.

The skrell were the most notable. A protected simian species, they were physically small, about half the stature of the Anunnaki. They were wary of the Anunnaki and not considered a threat. Although they had vocal cords, they were incapable of speech and were low in intelligence. However, they provided amusement with their antics and sometimes wandered through the lands surrounding the Anunnaki compounds and mining camps. Some were kept as pets or specimens for scientific study.

The skrell had a lifespan of forty Blue World years. In contrast, the Anunnaki, due to their knowledge of science and nutrition, had long ago eliminated death due to sickness and aging and were, in essence, immortal, except, of course, for any of them unlucky or foolish enough to suffer a catastrophic accident, like wandering into the blast zone of a transporter or starship. The Anunnaki also had the ability to go into a state of deep hibernation for over nine to-the-tenth culpi of time in order to survive periods of total deprivation.

The overhead lights began flashing, signaling that the time had come to descend. Enki and his contingent boarded the transporter. All wore their distinctive, black Shao capes. The Shao, from the planet of the same name, were a race of forest-dwelling bipeds that were worth less than their own hides, which were extremely pliable and comfortable, with excellent insulating properties.

The engines sighed and the transporter gently glided out of the brightly lit bay of the mother ship into the blackness of space. Enki wordlessly looked down upon the world they would live on. They would have to adapt, and in some ways it would be difficult. He frowned as he glanced at his officers. They all wore serious expressions, no doubt thinking similar thoughts. Nevertheless, Enki told himself, he and they were Anunnaki, and he was sure they would all acquit themselves well. For the next thousand revolutions of this gassy hunk of rock around its star, he would supervise and maintain the gardens that would sustain them in health during their stay. And he would also oversee the operation of the mines and the transport of gold on the cedar barges to where it would be stored in the temple tower to await shipment. He would enter the amounts in the ledgers and ensure that they met their quotas. And when the mother ship finally returned, the gold would be loaded, and Enki and the others would board and go home. Then the Blue World would be some other Commander's assignment.

Order was all, thought Enki, the key. That prime directive had been drilled into him practically from birth. And order must be maintained with an iron fist. That was the lesson from what had happened on another planet that orbits this star. Benri had once had a temperate climate, oceans and fertile landmasses. It had been populated by a simian race known as the Rook. Anu, the Great, had posted seven Anunnaki there to rule in his name. Over time they had grown corrupt and lax in their discipline. The Rook rebelled and took six of the seven Anunnaki prisoner. Then an enraged mob broke into the prison and chopped them into hundreds of pieces. The lone Anunnaki that had managed to escape in the transporter was found later orbiting the planet in a state of hibernation.

Anu's justice was slow in coming, but terrible in scope. A 100 kilometer in diameter asteroid traveling through space at 100,000 kilometers an hour, was steered into Benri, slamming into the planet with such force that it penetrated the internal magma, bulging the planet out on its other side. The planet's entire atmosphere instantly boiled off into space, killing all life there.

"Prepare for descent!" the pilot called. His face a frown of concentration, he entered his calculations into the computer, then worked the controls, turning the transporter for insertion. Enki strapped himself tighter into his seat as they began hurtling downward. Soon the ship shook violently as if invisible claws were attempting to tear its metal skin off. The vibration rose to a crescendo as they entered the planet's thick vapor clouds and it seemed as if the transporter would disintegrate from the atmospheric assault. Finally, they emerged into bright daylight and an eerie quiet engulfed them. Everyone stared in awe at the bright colors of the world below—grey granite rock, tan deserts, blue seas, jungles greener than a High Priest's gown.

The transporter dropped lower, skimming the roiling brown waters of a wide river. A lush jungle appeared below. Enki stared down through the porthole at the riot of brown branches and green leaves, red and violet flowers. A stepped, stone pyramid came into view, next to it the Eanna, or temple complex, and then the great stone blocks of the landing pad. The transporter stopped its forward movement and spiraled down the last few hundred feet, coming to rest with a gentle bump.

The doors hissed open. Enki and the other Anunnaki exited the transporter. The moment they were outside, they began coughing violently.

Enki's brother, Enlil, was doubled over. "How can we live here and breathe such foul gasses?" he cried as he looked sideways at Enki.

Before Enki could reply, someone came around a marble column and approached. The stranger bowed respectfully. "I am Danel," he said to Enki. "You must be my replacement, Enki."

Enki nodded between bouts of coughing. Enlil continued to cough and curse the Blue World as he tried to force its thick gasses into his lungs.

"The atmosphere is not normally this bad," said Danel. He pointed to a fire burning vigorously in some nearby trees. "Your engines ignited the vegetation. Soon it will burn out and the smoke will clear. Then you will all breathe easier."

"It does not seem to bother you," said Enlil.

"Of course not." said Danel. "I have grown used to the gases on this world, and so shall you."

"Of course," said Enki. He and the others continued to cough and look around at their new surroundings. After a few moments, the wind shifted slightly and Enki and his command followed Danel into the Eanna, which looked down on the verdant green of the gardens. The clouds they had seen when they'd first descended had moved on and the grid of the irrigated plains beyond reflected the sunlight like a vast mirror.

The following day was overcast, the vast watery plain below the Eanna obscured. Enki and his brothers spent their first day/night cycle on the Blue World resting and acclimating to the dense atmosphere. On the second day, when the sun was at its zenith, Enki assembled his staff in ranks opposite the departing contingent of Anunnaki. Danel, their commander, was the last to stride out. He saluted Enki, then gave a glowing speech lauding his own command for their hard work and esprit de corps.

Enki saluted Danel when he finished. Not to be outdone, he gave a long speech about Anunnaki tradition and history as the sun slowly descended behind the treetops in the west. He concluded by saying to all assembled, "Know this: The transition between Danel's most diligent stewardship and mine will be absolutely seamless. And when our assignment on this world comes to an end and the great Anu returns to take us home, he will be most highly pleased."

"Well spoken," said Danel, bowing. "I bid you farewell."

Danel and his command marched smartly away to the transporter. Enki and his brothers watched their fiery ascent.

As the roar of the engines faded, they became aware of another noise.

"Look!" said Enlil.

Across the canyon a troop of hairy skrell jumped and pointed at the quickly shrinking spacecraft, howling and shrieking. Enlil and the others laughed at their primitiveness and fear.

Enki and his lieutenants spent the next seven Blue World days inspecting the different facilities of the Anunnaki. Enki found the gardens in poor condition, with several canals and dikes broken, and many date palms and fruit trees dead and dying. Some of the livestock were too sick to be slaughtered for food. Enki and Enlil took a transporter flight to Shuruppak. Upon arriving, they found the air thin, hot and stinging in their nostrils. As they toured the mining operation, they discovered that the facilities and equipment were, like the gardens, in poor condition.

Enlil scoffed and shook his head in dismay. "Allowances will have to be made to the shipping schedule," he said, "to make up for the time that will be lost making repairs."

Enki agreed. "I am astonished that Danel, an Anunnaki commander, would have been so irresponsible."

"Well," said Enlil, "speaking of irresponsibility, you should have taken this tour before Danel departed."

Enki's frown was so slight as to be almost undetectable. The comment was typical of Enlil's jealous bickering and he chose to dismiss it. "That no longer matters. It is my command now and I will make things right."

"Of course, you will," said Enlil. "That is why our father chose you to command."

After many days of hard work, Enki had the mines and machinery back in working order. He looked through the porthole of the transporter as the crew ran through their checklist for the flight back to Eden. Anunnaki miners came and went from the main shaft, pushing their barrows before them. Soon all would be as it should, thought Enki. When the transporter landed at Eden, he immediately began the work of repairing the gardens, and culling and destroying the sick livestock.

For a time, Enki pondered the enigma of Danel's irresponsibility. He had never witnessed nor heard of any Anunnaki committing such a dereliction of duty. He wondered if perhaps the environment of the Blue World itself had somehow played a role. Could it have corrupted Danel? That seemed to him unlikely. Enki let it go. That was past. He decided that his tenure of command on the Blue World would be the complete opposite. And when Anu returned, his respect and gratitude would be boundless.

Enki devoted himself to bringing the gardens back to life. Together with his fellow Anunnaki, he tended and nurtured the trees and cattle until the operations returned to normal. Day followed day in a comforting blur of work, study and meditation. Over 500 such Blue World days passed blissfully when one day a shadow darkened the entrance to Enki's chamber. Enki looked up from his studying to see Enlil standing before him.

"Enlil!" said Enki excitedly. "I was so engrossed in my work I didn't even hear your ship landing. The flora of this world is endless, lush, prolific..." Enki shook his head in wonder. "It is seemingly beyond measure and I don't think I shall ever finish cataloging it all before it is time to go home."

Enlil's features were dark, and he said nothing in reply.

"What is it, Enlil?"

"I do not think we can make our mining quota this period," said Enlil.

Enki looked at him closely. "But the repairs have been made. And seventy-seven ingots every forty-nine days is not onerous. Even that scoundrel Danel managed that."

Enlil glowered. "The work in the mines is much harder than this..." He gestured dismissively at the plant specimens arranged about Enki's chambers. "...this gardening and record keeping. Twenty-one miners are simply not enough. You must provide more."

Enki looked out of the portal toward the green gardens shimmering in the distance. "Twenty and I to run the gardens, and eight left for transport and security... Can you not see I have no more to spare?" He turned back to Enlil, but his brother had gone. A few moments later Enki heard the roar of Enlil's transporter ascending. He went back to his studying and cataloging.

Enki met the next ore barge from Shuruppak at the quay. He inspected, finding only sixty-one ingots of gold, and they appeared to be poorly refined. Enki left the barge and put his assistant, Nuska, in charge of the gardens. He went to the transporter and ordered the pilot to take him to Shuruppak. When he arrived, he found the mining compound's buildings functional, but untidy. He visited the main shaft. According to the procedures there should have been eleven Anunnaki at work there; there were only five. Enki inspected the smelting plant and found the machines shut down and the furnaces cold to the touch. He left and went to find Enlil.

Laughter assaulted Enki's ears as he entered Enlil's chambers. Six Anunnaki miners played at a game of dice while Enlil studied a puzzle board before him. They looked up at Enki's entrance, their laughter coming to a halt.

"Brother," said Enlil, looking up, "what brings you to my command?" Enlil looked back down at his board game.

"Why are they not at work?" said Enki, pointing to the Anunnaki who had stopped their play.

Enlil looked at the shadow on the wall across from him. "I thought their shift had ended."

"No. Two hours more remain."

Enlil turned to the Anunnaki sprawled about in the room. They got to their feet. Casting dark looks at Enki, they left.

"So," said Enlil, "you flew out just to speak with me?"

"No. I will be staying in the small stone house at the end of the compound."

"For how long?" said Enlil, not looking up.

"You know how long, brother."

"I do?"

"For as long as it takes to establish discipline, order, and bring production back up to where it should be." Enki walked out of the chamber. Enlil scowled and looked back down at his puzzle board.

Two tens of days after Enki's arrival, ore production again rose back up to where it should have been. This freed Enki up to spend more of his time examining the flora and fauna of the savanna that bordered Shuruppak, an arid place that was very different from the balmy river-fed gardens of Eden.

On one of Enki's forays outside the compound, he came across a skrell cadaver. He took it back to the compound and performed an autopsy. He discovered that the creature was different than the skrell at Eden, with a slightly larger brain, and physically stronger. Internal burns indicated that it had died from an electrical discharge.

Enki went to a group of miners on their break. They looked up at his approach. "The skrell that I brought back to autopsy has internal burns indicating that someone smote it with their staff."

Their faces were defiant or blank. Then one stood, put down his bread, and said, "The creature climbed over the walls of the compound one evening and, instead of being scared off when confronted, continued advancing. Someone had had to strike it down with a jolt from their staff."

"Well," said Enki, "the protocols call for a mild, stunning shock first. Who was responsible?"

The miners looked at their feet. "I know not," said one. Others nodded in agreement. Enki decided to not pursue it, chalking it up to inexperience on the part of Enlil and his crew. He was more interested in the difference between this more intelligent and aggressive skrell than the ones at Eden. He decided to talk to Enlil further about the matter when he had time.

One hundred Blue World days passed in a blur of work and Enki decided that it was time to return to the gardens and resume his work there. Before he could announce his imminent departure, he was stirred from sleep one night by many shouting voices. He looked out his portal and saw flames rising from near the mine shafts. He got to his feet as the noise grew louder. Looking out, he saw torches as the miners approached his house.

"We will slave no more," an agitated voice cried out.

"No more!" others echoed.

Soon they were outside his door.

"Tell him!" a voice demanded.

"Yes, tell him now!"

"I will tell him."

Enki recognized his brother's voice. "Wait here," Enlil said to his fellow miners.

Enki heard Enlil's footfalls as he approached the door. Enki picked up his staff, illuminating his quarters. He opened his door. Enlil stood there, his miners arrayed behind him.

"Enki," said Enlil. "We will no longer work like animals."

"Enlil, I cannot believe what I'm hearing. Was this your idea?"

"Of course!" said Enlil with contempt. "Am I not in command here? Mining is tedious and back-breaking, not like your gentle work of gardening, counting and record keeping."

Enki heard the others shifting their feet behind Enlil.

"We will toil in the mines no longer!" muttered an angry anonymous voice. "It is exhausting and degrading."

"But," Enki called to those standing in the darkness behind Enlil, "the protocols are clear. We must extinguish our own self-centeredness for the good of all Anunnaki! Our father Anu has given us this assignment. His will must be done."

The shouts and jeers of those in the darkness drowned out Enki's voice.

Enlil turned and shouted at them. "Enough!" He turned back to Enki and jabbed a long ebony finger at him. "From this day forward you must do the work yourself, Enki. You and your assistants...for we are through."

Enlil turned to his fellows. "Come, let us go. We will slave in the mines no more."

The next day, Enki surveyed the camp. He found the blackened remains of the barrows and tools in a heap. The smelting kilns had been overturned but were salvageable. From inside the main building, Enlil and the others occasionally glared out at him in sullen anger and none of them would speak to him. Temporarily at a loss for what to do, he decided to return to Eden to think and plan.

For forty-eight days Enki attempted to negotiate an agreement with Enlil and the miners, but they put him off, still refusing to talk to him. On the forty ninth day the ore barge arrived. After discovering its empty hold, Enki began a fast and spent three days in the Anunnaki meditative state of ka searching for answers. The problem was Enlil, and those under his sway. They had become lazy. But Enki was responsible for motivating them, for production, for order. What could he do?

On the morning of the fourth day, as the Blue World star's golden rays crept into his chamber, Enki heard a commotion outside. He looked out to see a troop of skrell screaming in agitation. He shouted at them and they quieted. What could he do? There was work to be done, but not enough workers. He sat down and thought. Again, the skrell erupted in excited, insistent chattering, breaking his concentration. "Begone!" he shouted out the aperture. Silence settled down once again. The work in the mines must continue, Enki thought, but how? Who would do it? A skrell shrieked, shattering the silence.

Angered, Enki went out. Across the canyon from the Eanna, the skrell were pulling fruit from a tree. Looking around like thieves, they worked quickly and within mere minutes all the fruit within reach was gone. They sat on their haunches, cheeks stuffed roundly, as they gorged themselves. As Enki watched them, he had his answer. If Enlil and the other Anunnaki would not work the mines, then he, Enki, must create creatures that *would*. And the skrell would be his clay. He would use the stronger, more intelligent skrell from Shuruppak.

TWO

Since time immemorial the Anunnaki had seeded other worlds with life and used their scientific knowledge to genetically alter species. But Enki himself did not have the training to do this. He would have to employ the Hood of Knowledge. Most hominid life forms used only a tiny portion of their brains, but long ago the Anunnaki had developed the Hood of Knowledge to unleash the mind's full potential. The Hood contained the accumulated knowledge of the Anunnaki and would deliver that knowledge to the wearer. The Hood could also impart to the wearer the power to heal or to take life. But there was a price—the transformation sometimes caused excruciating pain, dizziness, and bleeding from the eyes, nose and ears. The knowledge would last only hours and would leave slowly with the pain. It was said that only Anu the Great retained all the knowledge without any side effects.

The protocols restricted the use of the Hood to Anu the Great and his priests, and only for the benefit of the Anunnaki. But, Enki reasoned, the accomplishment of his mission was solely for the benefit of the Anunnaki. And therefore, there should be no sanctions against him later.

After several days of fasting and meditation, Enki donned the Hood alone in his chambers. Despite a period of initial pain, several fascinating hours passed before he removed it, knowing exactly what he must do.

Enki took the transporter to Shuruppak and gathered Enlil and the other Anunnaki miners around him. He gestured to the quiet mine shafts and the machinery that still lay overturned around them. "I have found the answer to our problem," he said.

"*Your* problem," a miner in the back of the crowd shouted.

"Silence!" Enlil shouted. He addressed his brother. "What is the answer?"

"The skrell hold the answer."

Enlil and the assembled Anunnaki laughed with derision.

"Brother," said Enlil, "why do you waste our time with this nonsense. Those vermin can never be made to work. They are too stupid and wild."

Enki nodded in agreement. "Yes, Enlil, that is so. But I will put our mind into them and create a new species in our image."

The others began talking at once.

"But how can you do this?" someone shouted. "Only Anu and the priests have ever done such a thing!"

"Yes!" said others taking up the refrain, "only Anu the Great can work such wonders!"

Enki ignored the shouting. In a voice steely with resolve he said, "Yes, our father, Anu the Great...this is his will...and I will do it. Do you understand? His will is for seventy-seven ingots delivered to the Eanna every forty-nine days. It must be done." Enki pointed at the Anunnaki miner who had been shouting out, "And when he returns shall I tell him that you stood in the way of my efforts to carry out his will?"

The miners grew silent and cast their eyes downward. Enki turned back to Enlil. "The skrell here are bigger and stronger than those at Eden. They have larger brains. Go out and find a good male specimen. Stun it into unconsciousness but take care not to injure it. Then clean it up thoroughly with a salve and bring it to me."

The next day Enki and Enlil boarded the transporter to go back to Eden. At their feet lay a skrell, shocked into unconsciousness and trussed up securely.

***

Enki put the skrell into a deep sleep. He stuck an extractor into the creature's spleen. Enlil watched as Enki removed the creature's essence. Enki injected the essence into a beaker. He looked at Enlil.

"Give me your arm."

"Why?"

"Anu chose you to work the mines. If you will not work the mines, then those made in your image will."

Enki stuck the extractor into Enlil's arm and removed his essence. He then combined it with that of the skrell's in the beaker. He poured the contents into a vessel of protoplasmic material and put the mixture into the chamber. Three days later it had grown to full height and weight. Enki called it, the *Adam*—those bred to work.

From the moment Enki removed it from the chamber until he put it out of its misery, the Adam struggled against its restraints and howled like a vivisected skrell. Enki tried again. The second Adam lay semiconscious for three days before finally dying without a sound. Enki adjusted the variables and tried four more times with the same result. Enlil grew bored with the failures and wandered away.

Ten days later, Enki looked down on the seventh Adam. It had a strong pulse and was breathing regularly as it lay quietly on its slab. But, for two days it had not moved. Enki tried several different techniques to determine its perceptiveness. Even the shock he applied to its chest only caused its eyes to open briefly and glare into his own. Then its eyes closed, and he could rouse it no further. Enki decided it was brain-damaged like the others. He left his chambers to breathe the fresh air. When he returned an hour later, the Adam was gone.

Enki rushed outside to give the alarm. He saw no one about and descended the steps to the next level. He heard a commotion below and looked down. Two of the guards were dragging the struggling Adam back up the steps. It howled unintelligibly in rage as the guards shouted at it.

One of the guards looked up and saw Enki. He laughed, his face wide with wonder, "This creature almost made it over the wall. It is very clever and snuck right past us without making a sound!"

When the creature looked up and saw Enki, it threw itself down in abject fear, quaking and wailing.

"Lock it up for now," said Enki. "I will make more males and then females to breed them. When I have enough of both sexes for work details, we will begin training them."

Enki had only to create three female Adam to get one good specimen. He locked her up with the males and she mated with the strongest, but there were no offspring. After creating several more females, and placing them with the males, one showed signs of pregnancy. And so, Enki took that female and that male, and from them created seven pairs of Adam. Six pair he sent to Shuruppak with Enlil to begin breeding and working the mines, and one pair he kept with himself in his quarters atop the Eanna. He began teaching them all that they would need to understand and serve the Anunnaki. In the beginning it went well.

***

The male Adam snored heavily where he lay beside his mate on the straw mounded up inside their chamber. She nudged him and he awoke in the darkness. Misinterpreting her intent, he got atop her and pulled her close.

"No," she whispered. "We must go. Remember our plan?"

He grunted in acknowledgment and stood.

In the darkness, the soft pads of their feet made no sound as they walk along the giant stone blocks of the Eanna. He remembered all their sessions with Lord Enki. Always, only the Lord's silhouette was visible through the screen. His mighty voice rumbled as he taught them about this world that he had created for them and his own up in the heavens. He recalled the time when they had come upon the Lord as he sat alone in his chambers with his back to them—the lights in the golden crown atop his head shimmered with all the colors of the rainbow. Strangely, the Lord seemed unaware of them. They had started backing up, both sensing that this was something they were not permitted to see. But she had held back, wanting him to wait. They watched a little while longer. Days later when they lay together on their bed of straw, she spoke to him about what they had witnessed. "The crown of jeweled lights that graced the Lord's head was the Hood of Knowledge," she said. "I have overheard other gods speak of it. It is from the heavens and is what gives the Lord his great power." He nodded, his face grim with wonder and fear at the thought of it. "Later," she said, "we are going to take it and make ourselves as mighty as he."

They entered the chamber, dimly lit by glowing stones at its corners. She pointed and he saw the Hood sitting high above on its pedestal. He was surprised at its weight as he took it down and put it on. Pain immediately beset him as fiery images and noises raced through his head. He grabbed the pedestal to steady himself as the world spun dizzily around him. He pulled the Hood off and collapsed. Later, her scream woke him. He sat up to see her lying unconscious on the floor, the Hood on her head, as tears of blood streamed from her eyes. He knocked it from her. For several moments they lay together and held each other. Then the awful thunder of the Lord's angry voice came from everywhere at once. The room grew so bright that it pained their eyes and they had to cover them with their hands.

***

Nuska, Enki's assistant, stood at the doorway to his chambers. "They wait in the temple, Lord."

Enki nodded. He went outside and entered the temple. He saw them on the other side of the screen, kneeling, heads down and trembling. They had retained enough knowledge that they now felt shame and guilt. They had fashioned skirts for themselves out of the straw they slept upon.

"Why have you betrayed my trust?" he asked them.

The male looked at him with fear, saying nothing.

"So we could be like you, Lord," said the female. She wept bitterly.

Enki was unmoved by her tears. For them to think that they could rise to the same level as their creator by stealth and thievery— It was an affront!

Enki's voice thundered with anger, "You have broken my commandments!"

Both the male and female buried their faces in their hands and cried.

"Stand!" said Enki. "From this day forward you shall be banished from these gardens forever. You and all your issue will toil and live in the wildlands below. Begone!"

***

The Adam grew steadily in numbers and Enki soon used them to perform all the work in the gardens under the supervision of Nuska. At Shuruppak, on the plain, Enlil and his miners used the growing number of Adam to bring the production of gold up to the agreed-upon level. For a time, all went well. Then, once again, the numbers and quality of the ingots arriving on the barges deteriorated and Enki decided to move back to the mines for a time to supervise.

Enki, his entourage, and one of the Adam boarded the transporter for the flight to Shuruppak. Enki and the others took their seats. The ascent was routine. But when they began accelerating westward, Enki's nostrils flared at an unpleasant odor. He turned and saw the Adam crouching in fear on the deck by the door where he had shat himself. Enki frowned. Although the Adam were made in the image of the Anunnaki, and were vastly more advanced than the skrell, they were still primitives. He wished to improve them by further genetic manipulation, but Enlil had argued against it, fearing that if they became too intelligent, they would become more problematic. Things between Enki and Enlil were tense enough as it was, and so he had decided not to pursue it.

Upon arriving, Enki inspected the city that Enlil and his assistants had built next to the mines. A temple tower crowned its center and Enki took up residence there. The next day Enlil took him to inspect the mines and the living quarters of the Adam. They walked through the empty mud streets of the village past stick-walled, thatch-roofed dwellings hardly distinguishable from animal pens. Clouds of flies hovered here and there, and the air reeked of feces and wood smoke. They went to the hut of Bilou, the Adam that Enlil had trained and put in charge of the Adam miners. Without calling in to the inhabitants, Enlil boldly threw the door open and entered.

At the sight of Enlil and Enki, Bilou threw himself down on his knees. "Lord," the old Adam cried plaintively, "that you would enter my humble house... I am most honored."

"Stand," said Enlil, "and show us your working areas."

Bilou got to his feet. He led Enlil and Enki through the mines from one work site to the next, calling out loudly to all the Adam they came upon to avert their eyes.

Although Enki's intention had been solely to assess the operation of the mines, he could not help but take note of all they encountered. Back at Eden, he had no daily interaction with the Adam, having delegated their management in the gardens to Nuska. But his Adam workers were clothed, comely and generally quiet. Here the Adam seemed more primitive. Broad-browed, but hairless, unlike their simian ancestors, their facial features were coarse. They went about naked, having no shame. They had an unpleasant smell and their voices, although understandable, were not unlike the coarse barking of the skrell or the cacophonous chatter of the smaller tailed simians that climbed into the trees surrounding the temple at night. Enki and the Anunnaki were, in contrast, a handsome, reptilian race with finely chiseled noses and lips, elongated skulls, and eyes narrowed almost to slits from eons of evolution under the harsh glare of their star.

As they walked about, Ningish, one of Enlil's assistants, laughingly told Enki that the Adam referred to the Anunnaki as the walking serpents. Enki nodded as he stared at the Adam, marveling at the fact that a protocol forbidding sexual relations between the Anunnaki and other races had ever been thought necessary.

Completing his inspection, Enki concluded that the production problem was not one of insufficient infrastructure and labor, or even the Adam, but that Enlil was lazy, easily distracted, and not efficiently managing the Anunnaki and Adam under his command. After several hundred days of Enki's supervision, however, production was once again brought back up to where it should have been. During his time at Shuruppak, Enki also noted with concern that Enlil and the other Anunnaki often spent their evenings observing the activities of the Adam through the distance lenses that were placed about the walkways of the temple platform. Their interest was prurient and unseemly.

***

Enlil followed the old Adam, Bilou, along the path that snaked through the various work sites of the mines. Production had fallen somewhat, and he wanted to solve the problem before Enki got involved again. He and his brothers had had their fill of

Enki's interference and wished him gone back to his plants and studies at the Eanna.

An old female Adam, her bones bent from her labor, ran up to Enlil and Bilou. She cast her eyes down and said, "Lord, Bilou, please come! Someone is in great distress. You must speak to him."

Enlil and Bilou followed the female to where a crowd of Adam had gathered at an ore pit. The Adam fell back at the sight of Enlil. He saw a male squatting on his haunches, shaking in agitation as he drew lines in the dirt with a stick. Two females stood over him, attempting to calm him, but he would have none of it. Bilou went and spoke to the male softly. He returned to Enlil.

"Lord, his father died yesterday. Last night he had a dream in which his father appeared to him and told him that the walking serpents had struck his father down. He has told the other Adam to stop their work, for they too were doomed to die soon. Lord, forgive him, for in his grief he knows not what he is saying."

The male Adam pointed his stick at Bilou and said in a loud, accusatory voice, "You and the walking serpents have killed my father!"

The females continued to try and calm the Adam, but he raged on, "Bilou is a traitor to us all!"

The male stood, turning around to shout at the crowd, "even now Bilou plots with the walking serpents. They will soon slaughter us like sheep!"

Worried muttering rippled through the crowd.

Enlil turned to Bilou. "Tell them to return to their work."

Bilou raised his arm for silence. "Lord Enlil commands you to return to your work."

The tumult did not subside. The male turned to point at Enlil and Bilou. "We must rid our world of the walking serpents and their pets." He turned to the Adam around him, "and we must start with these two."

The male started advancing toward Enlil and Bilou. The crowd followed with slow, tentative steps.

Enlil raised his arms. "Go back, I command thee!"

The crowd paused, but the male continued to advance.

Enlil raised his staff. A pulse of millions of joules of energy arced through the air like a lightning bolt and the male exploded in light and smoke. The smoke slowly drifted away, revealing a pillar of glowing ash. The remaining Adam screamed in fright and threw themselves onto the ground, covering their eyes as they wailed.

Enlil scowled at Bilou. "That vermin like this would think they could ever subvert my command... It is outrageous! A lesson had to be taught to them!"

Bilou bowed in subservience.

Enlil looked back at the crowd of Adam. "Silence!" he roared in a voice as loud as a waterfall.

When the Adam quieted, he continued, "I am your lord, Enlil, ruler of this world, and this is what will happen to any who disobey my commandments."

Enlil waited for his words to sink in. He continued, "Let it be known among you that any who disturb this pillar of ash shall suffer the same fate."

Enlil turned and nodded to Bilou.

Bilou raised his arms. "Rise!" he exhorted the Adam. "Rise and leave this place. Go back to your work."

Slowly the Adam turned and walked back into the ore pit.

***

Enki soon heard about what Enlil had done and went to see for himself. On the way he spotted several Adam through the trees, but they went well out of their way to avoid him. Once, at a turn in the trail, a male came upon him and fell down in a faint. Enki knelt to him and probed his mind, removing any memory of the encounter. When the Adam regained consciousness later, all that would remain would be faint dream-like images.

Enki came to the pit where Enlil had smitten the Adam. The faint odor of burnt flesh hung in the air. Despite the head having toppled off, the heap of ash was still recognizable as an Adam. Enki frowned in distaste. The Adam were his creation and were primitives. Still, he would have handled the situation differently. This had not been necessary, and he had said as much to Enlil. He had scoffed and walked off.

Enki left the pit. He decided to search for new botanicals. When not supervising the mining operations, he enjoyed his exploratory walkabouts, studying the many variations of life on the chaotic Blue World—the riotous explosion of fauna at the river banks and the oasis, the insects and reptiles, mammals as small as a finger and as large as a house. But it was the Adam that intrigued him the most, and not because they were his creation. They were very hardy, like the bright green weeds that pushed up between the house-sized granite blocks of the landing pad. Noisy, brutish, and stupid, they were given only to eating, fornicating, and brawling. And if he had not given them laws and forced them to work, they would have already wiped each other out and disappeared from the planet. Enki had observed a female leave her offspring unattended in the bushes while she was mounted by a particularly aggressive male. A large canine carried her baby off and devoured it hurriedly and hungrily. No matter— Three months later the same female was already showing signs of carrying another. The Adams' squabbles and feuds were never-ending. Enki witnessed brother smite brother. For tens of days he observed an Adam peacemaker who had achieved some stature and a following. Then one day he was lured deep into the forest where his brains were bashed out. Simple, beastly primitives in every way, yet a testament to the life force in all things, low and mighty. The Adam were very fertile, quickly growing in number. And most importantly, although they occasionally needed to feel the sting of the whip, they were capable of hard laboring all day. The mines would still be shut down if not for them.

After a while, Enki put the enigma of the Adam out of his mind. The Anunnaki priests could puzzle over such things. His assignment was to ensure order and to keep the mines and the gardens operating day and night. This he did. Time passed and the mines produced on schedule. All was good. Then one night a hurried knocking woke him.

Enki opened his door. An Anunnaki guard stood before him.

"Lord Enki, the Adam called Bilou is at the gates. He says that many of the Adam are unable to rise from their beds. They burn with fever and their bowels run continuously."

Enki nodded wordlessly as he put on his cape. Later, he and Bilou walked through the mud-filled streets of the Adam village. Bilou paused and gestured at a row of hovels. "All of these, Lord. Very sick."

Enki nodded and they entered the first. A female lay in the bed, semiconscious. A male squat by her side, shaking his head in lament.

"Send him away," Enki said to Bilou.

After the male left, Enki rubbed the female down with disinfectant and lifted her into his arms. He carried her back up to the temple platform, leaving Bilou at the gates.

Anunnaki medicine had no effect on the female and Enki was unable to revive her. She died within an hour. Enki opened her up and found her lungs full of fluid. He incinerated her and went back with Bilou to bring another dying subject up, a male. He removed a sample of its blood, and after analysis, discovered a parasitic invasion. The subject's white blood cells had multiplied many times over to fight off the sickness, to no avail. And again, despite the administration of other powerful Anunnaki medicines, this subject also died quickly. Enki was in the process of dissecting him when Enlil entered the chamber.

"Brother," said Enlil, "half of the Adam are unable to work." His tone indicated no alarm, but rather that he was merely reporting a problem— Enki's, not his own.

Enki continued to inspect the diseased organs of the Adam on the table before him. "I know. I am working on the problem now."

"The other Adam refuse to enter the pits and the mining operation has almost come to a halt." Enlil scoffed. "They say that evil spirits hover in the air there, waiting to attack them."

"I have heard all of this already," said Enki. "Leave me to my work."

Enlil ignored him and remained standing. "And the time draws nigh, Brother."

Enki's concentration began to wane. He could not hide his irritation as he looked up at Enlil. "The time?"

"The thousand days, Brother. Soon the mother ship will return, and we will leave this place."

Enki said nothing as he went back to examining the specimen before him.

"Brother," said Enlil, "we will soon leave. Why do you bother with these verminous creatures? Let them die."

"Leave me!" Enki muttered.

Enki took the transporter to the jungles bordering the mining areas. He thought of his brother's words. To Enlil, the Adam might be vermin, but they had become essential to the operation of the mines and gardens, *Enki's* operations, *his* command. And he was not going to stand before Anu later and admit that he had allowed that operation to slow down and come to a stop.

Enki held his staff at the ready for predators as he walked the path through the trees and bushes. If the medicine of the Anunnaki had no efficacy here, then perhaps the flora of the Blue World contained a cure. He knelt and began collecting botanical samples, occasionally looking around and behind. He brought dozens of plants back to his quarters. All day he labored to turn them into compounds. Over the next several days he injected them into the sick Adam. But they had no effect and the Adam continued to die in great numbers. One male he had carried up to his quarters slipped into a coma before Enki could minister to him. As Enki lay him down, the male regained consciousness and grabbed Enki's cape with an iron death grip. He looked deep into Enki's eyes. "Lord," he cried, "have mercy!" Something seemed to leap across the void between them and Enki felt a tiny ache inside, as if some microbe or spore had sunk its needle-like roots into his core. The Adam's eyes closed, and it died.

Enki brought several more Adam to his chambers to treat, with no effect. Soon he grew discouraged. He sat motionless, exhausted. As an Anunnaki, he had never been confronted with a sickness that could not be cured in a heartbeat. But if such a sickness had affected his Anunnaki brothers, he would have entered the inner sanctum of the Eanna and donned the Hood of Knowledge. He had used the power of the Hood to create the Adam, an act he thought he could defend before Anu as having been necessary to perform his mission. But to don the Hood again— Perhaps Enlil was right. Their mission might be doomed. And they would be leaving this world soon anyway.

"No!" Enki said, rallying himself, "I am in command." He continued his efforts to cure the Adam. Days upon days followed and he had no success. He began watching the skies nightly, dreaming of the arrival of the ship. Perhaps his replacement could solve this problem, or perhaps Anu. It seemed beyond his power.

Enki descended into the Anunnaki meditative state of ka. For seven days he floated in a boundless pool of blackness, telepathically communicating with the denizens of other worlds. But the intellects he encountered had nothing to offer him. He entreated and rested, entreated and rested, crying out for answers. On the seventh day he raised himself. He had learned only that he could not cease his efforts to solve the problem. He could never face Anu and admit that he had given up. He must go back into the forests and collect more botanical specimens.

Enki brought more of the dying Adam back to his chambers to inject his new compounds into them. The result was always the same—they would die within the hour. He took the transporter further out and noticed a tree he'd never seen before, laden with verdant, drooping branches and leaves. Back at his quarters, he made a compound of the leaves and injected it into a dying Adam. It seemed to have an effect. The rapid climb of the subject's temperature slowed. Enki administered more of the compound and the subject's fever began to break. Soon the Adam regained consciousness and sat up. Enki gave him a bowl of gruel and he hungrily fed himself. Several hours later the Adam had made a complete recovery and fell to his knees in prayer before Enki.

Enki led the healed Adam to the gate. They met Bilou and took the transporter deep into the forest to gather up several bales of the leaves. Back at Enki's chambers, they made more of the compound. They then went to the Adam village. They put the compound into the wells. Within a day, many of the Adam began to regain their health. Within the span of seven days all had recovered and were once again working in the pits and ore-processing centers and the local gardens.

As the sun set behind the distant hills, Enki watched a gold-bearing barge move slowly down-river toward the sea. He was very pleased. Now he looked upon the Adam differently. He had an affection for them, born of their quiet suffering and his time and effort to alleviate it, and their sincere gratitude. There was something else he now saw in them, something akin to pride, nobility, worth. Could it be? Whatever it was, it was good, and the Blue World days again began to pass like moments.

***

Morning brought the beautiful aroma of blooming flowers and the chirping of birds. Enki heard the scratch of sandaled feet at the entrance to his chambers. It was Enlil.

"Brother," said Enlil. "The time for the mother ship to arrive is now."

Enki sat up. Drunk with sleep and still feeling the glow of his victory over the disease, he slowly became aware of the frustration and anger in his brother. He thought it best not to be drawn into it. "Have there been any messages from the mother ship?"

Enlil's face was dark and angry. "No!" he spat. "The transceiver is quiet and cold. There is nothing."

Before Enki could say anything further, Enlil turned and went away.

Ten days later, on the day of their scheduled departure from the Blue World, Enki's brothers changed notably. While Enki continued to go about his duties, monitoring the Adam in the mines, his lieutenants and engineers became sullen and lazy. He tried to reassure them, insisting that the mother ship would soon return.

"No," they exclaimed, "the contract has been broken!" This was something that had never happened before. Enki tried to raise their spirits, but they would not listen to him.

One night as Enki walked along the edge of the temple grounds to enjoy the cool air, he came upon Enlil and some others arguing heatedly in the dark. When they saw him approach, they grew silent.

"A beautiful night," said Enki. "The sky is full of stars and the air cool from the shower we had earlier."

Enlil grunted in reply and the others remained silent. After Enki left them, they began talking again in soft tones. He heard someone say, "But surely, Anu would never desert us."

Enlil spat. "You are a fool. How can you..."

Enki walked back to them. "Enlil," he said into the dimness, "remember, we are Anunnaki, sons of Anu the Great."

Enlil's silence hung in the air like a bad smell.

"I will brook no slanderous talk in my command," Enki continued. "Do you understand?"

"Yes," Enlil said finally.

Enki walked away. He knew that his admonition had not changed Enlil's heart. What could he do to restore Enlil's and the others' sense of pride and duty as Anunnaki, sons of Anu the Great?

The days passed swiftly and the mines continued to produce on schedule, and so Enki stopped fretting over Enlil and the others. But they grew increasingly bored with their lives in the temple atop the tower and bolder in their resentment.

Five hundred more days passed without the return of the mother ship. Enki noted that Enlil and the others no longer spent their evenings angrily denouncing Anu and their mission here. Instead they began to take a growing interest in the daughters of the Adam down on the plain. Enki often saw them watching the Adam through the distance lenses. Enlil seemed more interested than most. He watched the same female every night as she bathed. He'd even given her a name. Occasionally, Enlil's and the others' talk would drift through the portal of Enki's chambers. They talked of which ones they found comely, and their habits.

The passage of time emboldened Enki's brothers and they made little attempt to hide their talk from him. Sometimes in the darkness, when they could no longer see the plain, they would loudly discuss their favorite Adam females. And although the protocols forbade physical contact with the Adam, they began to speak loudly and openly of their desire for such, reveling in the details as each one attempted to surpass the other with lewd talk.

Enki grew more isolated and concerned. Every night he would stare up at the blackness, hoping to see a bright new star overhead signaling the arrival of his father in the mother ship. But there was nothing. One night, overcome with sadness, Enki cried out into the black heavens, "Father! Why have you abandoned us?"

Warm moist air perfumed with the scent of flower blossoms teased Enki's nostrils as he drifted in a state of ka, debating a great, tentacled creature about the origins of the universe. Bold footsteps scratched along the stones outside his quarters, bringing him quickly back up to consciousness. He got to his feet as Enlil and some of the others entered his chamber. Enlil glared at him.

"Why have you come?" said Enki.

"What do you think?" said Enlil.

Enki slowly shook his head, "To go down to the plain would be against the protocols. There would be chaos."

The others said nothing for a moment. Encouraged, Enki quickly said, "We are Anunnaki! We are above that."

"We are abandoned," said Enlil flatly, "that is what we are."

"Aye, abandoned," someone said. Several others grumbled in agreement.

"Our father has given us our orders and assignments," said Enki.

"We wish to re-negotiate the orders," said Enlil, "with you."

"I will negotiate nothing with you," said Enki. "I take orders only from our father, Anu, the Great, Lord of the Universe. Must I one day report to Anu that you have disobeyed his orders?"

Enlil glared at Enki for a few moments. Then he turned and left, the others following him.

The next day, Enlil and the other Anunnaki returned to their duties. But after several tens-of-days their work slowed, and they spent more and more of their time watching the Adam below through the lenses and talking loudly in lewd terms. After several tens of days, they again entered Enki's chamber.

"What is it this time?" said Enki, knowing full well what they wanted.

Enlil spoke for the others. "It is now one thousand and nine hundred days since we came to this world, and still there is no ship, no word."

"It is so," said several lieutenants behind him.

Enki stared at them, his face blazing with anger. "What would you have me do?"

Enlil laughed. "Nothing! There is nothing you can do. And there is nothing we can do. We have decided that from now on we are not bound by the protocols. If you wish, we will put into writing that this was our decision alone, and that you opposed it."

Enki's voice thundered with rage. "To abandon the protocols is to invite chaos! It is written!"

"Our principals have abandoned us," said Enlil. "We have decided."

Enki inwardly railed at what he was hearing. But he knew he was beaten. "Put it in writing then," he said. "Now leave me." He turned away.

Enlil and the others went out.

Enki stared at the chamber wall for a long time. What could he do to stop this? Nothing. "Father!" he cried out, "all mighty Father... why have you abandoned us?"

And so, it happened that Enlil and the other Anunnaki went down to the plain and lay with the female Adam. Many of them built houses of stone on the plain and lived there with their females. Others brought their females up to the temple tower to live. The union of the Anunnaki and Adam was fruitful and soon their offspring, which they called the Human, could be seen running and playing on the plain and in the gardens. They soon grew to adulthood and begat offspring of their own.

THREE

Enlil and the rebel Anunnaki gave to their Human offspring the knowledge of weaving, architecture, metallurgy, the smithing of swords, knives, shields and breastplate, the wheel, viticulture and winemaking. Eventually the Human came to look down upon the primitive Adam. They killed many of them and drove the rest into the forests and surrounding mountains where they disappeared over time. The extended families of the Human grew in numbers and wealth and became independent tribes with their own city-states upon the plain, each with an Anunnaki god-king. Enki, who had long returned to the Eanna at Eden, looked upon these developments with abhorrence because all of it was forbidden by the protocols. But Anu had never returned and so it went unpunished.

Enki confined himself to the Eanna and continued to follow Anu's orders. Under Enki's diligent guidance, the Human workers kept the mines and gardens in efficient operation. For a long, long time Enki suffered no ill effects from his separation from his brothers. Then one day he called for his assistant, Nuska, to discuss the progress of a new canal they were building. Not receiving an answer, he went to Nuska's chambers and discovered that he too had abandoned his post to live on the plain in one of the new Anunnaki Kingdoms. Despite the loss, Enki continued to enjoy the quiet and time he had for learning and meditation. But the longer it went on, the more the absence of Anunnaki voices bothered him. He didn't understand this new feeling, or the feeling he got when his footsteps upon the cold stones of the Eanna reverberated back on him from all quarters. Was someone there, he would wonder hopefully. Then he would stop and listen, his ears catching nothing. Why should this bother him? He was living according to the protocols. He was true to Anu. He was honorable. But it did bother him, and he finally left the vast solitude of the Eanna.

Enki moved down onto the plain. He built a house at the edge of the forest. Now the lush life and distractions of the Blue World were all around him every hour of the day and night. The endless sights and sounds mitigated his boredom. Because he was now geographically closer to the Human, he could observe them surreptitiously as they went about their business. He discovered that because of further infusion of Anunnaki DNA due to the violations of the protocols by Enlil and the other Anunnaki, the Human were now vastly more attractive and intelligent than the Adam had been.

Enki's duties took up less and less of his time and he spent more of it in the state of ka. But something had changed within him and he began to find it more and more difficult to draw other intelligent minds to his own for intercourse. Soon his meditations grew empty and he stopped them. To fill the long days and nights, he spent even more time observing the Human as they grew in numbers and sophistication. And during that time, they learned of his presence. While out collecting botanical samples, he felt someone's eyes upon him. He circled around the offender and came upon her in a clearing. She was a golden-haired beauty. And there was something else that caused Enki's eye to linger on her—her boldness. She made signs for him to approach. He felt a mixture of attraction and revulsion. The protocols may have been abandoned by the others, but not by him. He raised his staff as if to smite her and she ran away.

Afterward she kept a distance from him, but her interest in him did not wane. And, despite himself, Enki continued to watch her from afar. But, he told himself, only for the sake of research and science.

***

A knock came on Enki's door. He opened it.

Enlil stood there. "Brother," he said, "I see you have finally come to your senses and abandoned the Eanna."

"I have abandoned nothing, Enlil. That is your sin, and the others'. I have merely moved my residence down here to be closer to the flora and fauna."

Enlil laughed deep in his throat. "Ah, the fauna, eh? You have not changed."

Enki said nothing, smarting at the taunt.

"I and the others," said Enlil in a haughty voice, "wanted to invite you to view a great battle which is about to take place. My Human forces will engage the forces of Samyaza in the Valley of the Kings. I have set up a comfortable place for viewing. Will you come?"

As Enki looked at his brother, he thought about how widespread and grotesque the chaos has become. He shook his head. "No, Enlil. What value is there in such slaughter? Is it for science? Is it to save another species? No. it is merely for your enjoyment. Of course I will not attend."

Enlil laughed. "Very well. But, Enki, your isolation is not healthy. Surely you are not content to sit in this house by yourself day after day when you could be enjoying the fellowship of the other Anunnaki and the pleasures of the Human females."

"I have work I must do," Enki snapped. "I have no more time for such talk."

Enlil nodded, a thin smile on his lips. "Very well, my brother. I should have known I could not change a mind as strong as yours. But I have one more request."

Enki waited.

"I want to take you a short distance from here and show you something I know you'll be interested in."

They left Enki's house and Enki pulled the stone door closed. "Very well. Let us be off."

Enlil led the way through the forest along a thin path that Enki had not known about. The path led upward. After some distance, Enki's ears caught the sound of splashing water. Soon they came out of the trees onto a rocky outcropping overlooking a valley beyond dotted with villages and fields of barley and other grains. Just below them was a pool of inviting water fed by a nearby waterfall.

Enlil waved his arm to take in the entire panorama. "All of this could be yours, Enki."

Enki said nothing as he watched some Human drive a herd of cattle across the plain, raising a trail of tan dust.

"Aknan is departing for what he sees as better lands on the jungle continent. These lands could be your own kingdom if you wanted."

Enki turned to his brother and shook his head in disgust. "I have already told you how I feel about abandoning our protocols and disobeying our father." He turned to go.

"Wait," Enlil said. "There is more." Enlil pointed. In the pool below, a naked female Human had waded out to bathe. Enki recognized her as the golden-haired beauty that had been watching him. He could not turn away and stared as if rooted like a tree. She laughed as she walked through water up to her knees, calling out to someone hidden in the bushes.

"I know you have been watching her," said Enlil. "She could be yours alone."

Enki felt that he must get away, but he could not take his eyes off her. "It is against the protocols," he said vaguely.

Enlil laughed. "Whose protocols? Those who have abandoned us upon this steamy hunk of rock? Enki, the protocols mean nothing now. Surely you have come to know that. Now we must all adapt. We must make the best of our abandonment and take what simple pleasures this primitive planet offers."

***

Kish felt eyes upon her as she washed her long hair in the pool. She warmed initially, thinking it might be Lord Enki, but then grew doubtful. Despite leaving offerings of flowers and fruits at his door, he stayed away. The others said that he no longer lived in the small temple by the edge of the forest, but she hoped he did, for she believed he had some interest in her.

Shaking her long blonde hair, then wringing it out as best she could, she waded out of the pool. Over the soft splash of the falls she heard her friend, Melish, call her.

Melish stepped out from behind some bushes and they picked up the load of reeds that they had gathered earlier to weave into baskets. They entered the forest and walked down the dimly lit trail. Overhead, birds and monkeys kept up a steady racket.

"Did you see Meskag today?" Kish asked her friend as they walked.

Melish smiled and nodded, her hand unconsciously going to her already swollen belly. She and Meskag were a pair now and would move in together as soon as Meskag got permission from his overseer.

After they had walked a while, Kish paused.

"What is it?" asked Melish.

"Do you hear it?"

"What?" said Melish.

"The quiet. The birds and animals are silent."

Melish frowned with concern as she looked around at the darkening green of the forest pressing against them.

"Come," said Kish. "Let us go on before night falls."

The two women had not gone far when they heard something in the bushes ahead off to the side of the trail. They stopped.

The dark form of the god, Enlil, shook the foliage, knocking down a stand of brush with a wave of his muscled arm. He stepped out onto the trail. Both women immediately knelt, bowing their heads.

"You!" said Enlil in a deep, frightening voice.

They looked up. He pointed at Melish. "You! Go away."

Melish bowed. She got to her feet and backed off, hurrying down the trail the way they had come.

"Look at me!" Lord Enlil commanded Kish.

Kish looked up to see him standing over her. She saw his excitement and she was afraid. "No, Lord. Please."

Enlil pushed her head down and ignored her cries as he mounted her from behind. He was rough and quick with her and she did not like it. When he finished, he said, "From now on, whenever I want you, never dare refuse me or it will be the last thing you do."

Temporarily unable to speak, Kish hung her head.

Melish returned in the twilight and found Kish sitting on the trail where she had left her. Wordlessly, she helped her to her feet. Together they gathered up the load of reeds and hurried to get home before darkness fell.

***

Days passed and the strange new malady of loneliness began to plague Enki. It grew so great that one day he could not rise from his bed. He longed to hear the voices of the Human, to watch them. He even found himself longing to talk with his Anunnaki brothers. Finally, he got up and went out into the forest. He searched for most of the day before he found the female with the golden hair and brought her home as his slave.

Her name was Kish. Enki could not bring himself to violate the protocols further by lying with her, but he taught her how to manage his house. Kish learned well and the arrangement was good. And so, Enki spent his days in the mines and gardens and returned to his house most evenings. He taught Kish how to prepare his food in the Anunnaki manner. After she fed him, he would retire to his own chamber to rest and achieve ka. Although he had little interaction with Kish, just having her in his house helped dispel his loneliness. But then another malady began to plague him—longing. He often found himself thinking of her. He fought it, but his unconscious mind contrived reasons for interacting with her. And he held her gaze much longer than necessary.

An unseasonably cold winter descended on the plain. Enki used the deep cold and the short days, and especially his work, as a brace to fight the longing. For a while it worked. Then spring arrived, seemingly overnight. A warm rain fell for days, then hot and balmy nights that seemed everlasting. Thousands of fruit trees in the gardens of Eden flowered simultaneously, releasing their sweet aroma into the breeze. Every night, the hot, perfumed air filled Enki's chamber, permeating every pore of his body, intoxicating him. For weeks he lay in his bed, unable to think, unable to achieve ka, unable even to sleep. One night, in a daze, he found himself in Kish's chambers, looking down upon her. She opened her eyes and met his gaze, unafraid. She gave herself to him willingly and afterward he fell into a deep sleep. The next day Enki moved her into his chambers.

Kish bore Enki a son whom he named Gamilesh. Now that Enki had broken the protocols against lying down with other species, a strange calm descended upon him. He had crossed a threshold, and nothing happened. There was no turning back. Days flew by, seasons came and went. Enki could never undo what had been done on the Blue World, but he believed that by continuing with his duties he could perhaps, when his father arrived, plead with him for mercy. And so, he made sure the gardens' harvests were regular and bountiful and the cedar barges continued to arrive from the mines full of gold and other metals to be added to the growing mounds in the temple storehouses. The Blue World circled its heavenly star and Gamilesh was followed by another son, Nergal. Soon thereafter, Enki's house echoed with their laughter and talk. He was fascinated by the abilities of his wife, Kish. He taught her the science of botany and how to weave. Their dwelling soon filled with a riot of beautiful plants, and the cloth she wove had a wild, unsymmetrical beauty that he found almost on a par with Anunnaki design. Although Kish had never been trained in Anunnaki ways, she instinctively knew how to raise their children. With a smile or a word, she could inflate them with pride, and with a frown or a turned back, reduce them to tears—to be forgiven and raised up later when she deemed the lesson had been learned. Her intuitive nature and intelligence were uncanny. He had never believed the Human capable of such things. Was it the infusion of Anunnaki essence or the mysterious naturalness of the Blue World? No matter. Someday perhaps he would understand, but for now he simply accepted it.

Enki loved both his sons, but it was Gamilesh that pleased him the most. Unlike his brilliant, but passive younger brother, Nergal, Gamilesh was playful and aggressive, with an inquisitive streak that bubbled up in endless questioning and experimentation. When Gamilesh was but ten years of age, Enki took him and Nergal aboard the transporter for the trip to Shuruppak. As they lifted off, the Human laboring in the fields stopped to watch their fiery ascent with wide-eyed, open-mouthed astonishment. Nergal clung fearfully to his mother's gown during the ascent, while Gamilesh watched the pilot's every move with the eyes of a hawk.

***

Gamilesh, son of the god Enki, and his friend Erdu, son of Lesh, one of the gods who oversaw the operation of the vineyards, stood on the hillside, the warm breeze moving their long hair as they stared down at the temples. Entry to the temples was forbidden to the Human, but Gamilesh had once been taken inside by his father when he was much younger. Gamilesh remembered the fear he'd felt when the ground under his feet had seemed to rumble with the voice of the great old one, Anu, father of the gods.

"I have been inside the temple and I have heard the voice of Anu," said Gamilesh. "I swear to it."

Erdu, frowned. "You do not have to swear." He pointed to the amulet hanging around Gamilesh's neck—a tiny golden replica of the thunderbirds the gods flew to Baalbek and other mountain bases. "You say that you and Anu will converse. If he does not speak, will you give that to me?"

Gamilesh's brows compressed in earnestness. "Of course."

They crept down the hill, keeping to the cover of the bushes and trees. Halfway down, seeing no one about, they ran till they were a stone's throw from one of the smaller Anunnaki temples. They hid behind some bushes. The rectangular structure had reed walls and a reed-thatched roof. A golden pike with a serpent wrapped round its length protruded from the roof. Gamilesh had already told Erdu that the pike was a 'tongue,' extending from the golden sarcophagus, from which emanated the voice of Anu.

An Anunnaki guard came around the building and paused. He stared straight ahead, occasionally looking left and right.

"How will we get inside with him there?" Erdu asked.

Gamilesh was about to reply when a tremendous roar rent the afternoon quiet. He and Erdu watched an Anunnaki transporter thunder skyward from the Eanna atop the mountain.

They looked back down at the Anunnaki guard, his head moving as he followed the course of the flying machine. When the din receded Gamilesh said, "I have watched him before. He always goes away around this time to take a shit in the woods. We will have enough time to go inside and have a look."

Erdu nodded. "Good." He grabbed the little golden thunderbird hanging around Gamilesh's neck. "Let me see it again." He turned it about as he studied it.

"Look!" said Gamilesh, pointing down, "I told you."

They looked down to see the guard walking off.

"Come," said Gamilesh.

They ran and slipped quickly inside the temple. It was hotter inside, dryer, and a soothing hum filled the quietness. Gamilesh felt something in the air tickling his scalp, like before a thunderstorm. Closed off behind a red, waist-high wooden railing, the sarcophagus was bigger than two men, one atop the other. Made of gold, it had silver hoops encircling it every hand's breadth up its length, ending in a golden pike sticking up and through the roof. It seemed to shine with a light all its own. They stared at it in awe.

"Why is it not speaking?" said Erdu.

"I do not know," said Gamilesh, "Let us wait a little longer." He went back to the entry door to see if the guard had returned. Erdu climbed over the railing. Gamilesh turned back to see him approaching the sarcophagus. Before Gamilesh could tell him not to, the other boy laid his hand upon one of the silver rings. A mighty groan emanated from the sarcophagus as Erdu's hair erupted in flame, and smoke shot from his eyes, ears and mouth. He collapsed into a small heap of smoking cloth. Along with the smoke, a terrible smell filled the chamber. Gamilesh cried out with grief. Moments later a large hand seized him.

Kish looked up from where she sat on her couch, her eyes wet with tears. Gamilesh sat beside her as they waited for Enki to arrive. Gamilesh hung his head in shame as his father entered the chamber.

Enki addressed himself to Kish. "I have made arrangements for Gamilesh to live in Bad-tibira and study the construction of the barges under Nuska's tutelage." Enki turned to his son. "Leave us."

Gamilesh walked down the stone corridor, his fists balled into his tear-filled eyes.

Later Kish said in an anguished voice to Enki, "Why? Why?"

Enki stood, facing away from her. "He knew my rules and wishes. Yet he chose to disobey them."

"Yes," said Kish, "he was foolish, but he asked for your forgiveness."

"Yes, and I forgive him. But sometimes I do not understand him, as if he is no son of mine. He is too bold for a Human."

"He is young."

Enki turned to her. "He is almost grown. And he needs more discipline, study, and work. I will speak no more of it."

***

Many days passed and the sons of Enki and Kish grew and took wives. When Gamilesh arrived at Eden on the gold-bearing barges, he now brought his wife and their son, Zeb and daughter, Anot. And Gamilesh's brother Nergal and his wife Peshta and

their son, Nabi, and daughter, Peshmer, also visited Enki and
Kish. Enki's life now had a dimension he never knew
existed—happiness. He had known discipline, work,
achievement, mastery, and pride, but never happiness. And this
new phenomenon was coupled with the unhappy knowledge
that the very things that gave him happiness were growing old
and moving quickly toward their end of days, while he remained
relatively unchanged by Blue World time. He could not stop the
aging of his wife and children and grandchildren by donning
the Hood of Knowledge, for that was forbidden. But he could
use his knowledge of medicine and the natural processes and
bounty of the Blue World to slow it down. And so, he taught
them all he knew about which fruits and herbs to eat to ensure
health and slow aging. Soon Gamilesh was training his son Zeb
in the construction and operation of the gold-bearing barges,
and Nergal was training his son in the arts of astronomy and
mathematics. Kish helped train her granddaughters in the arts
of weaving and tapestry, and that most difficult of feminine arts,
how to control the outcome of things while feigning
submissiveness and inaction.

On the plain, all the Human clans grew vastly in number,
and for a time Enki thought the chaos he had feared had
somehow been avoided. Could the Anunnaki teachings be
wrong? But then a hint of the chaos appeared. Some of the
unions of the Anunnaki and Human produced monsters. Due
to some unknown anomaly, thirteen children were born with
deformed facial features. They grew to enormous proportions,
some of them over nine cubits in height, and were called giants.
Enlil and the other Anunnaki wanted to destroy them, but Enki
decided to take advantage of their great size and strength. He

taught them the art of masonry and had them build great stone temples, gates and monuments. But, even the normally proportioned Human were not without problems. There were occasional wars, work stoppages in the gardens and mines, and murders of passion. Many of the young males slipped out of their assigned villages in the evenings to tryst with females from other villages. Several had been struck down dead by the fiery swords of the Anunnaki guards when they attempted to sneak back in before sunrise.

The Blue World spun out its days and nights. One evening Enki came into his house after supervising the relocation of some fruit trees. Kish stood before the mirror, her face dark.

"What is it?" he said.

She brushed out her long locks with her hand and turned to him. "Children...grandchildren...I am growing old."

"Yes. What of it?"

"Do you still find me pleasing to look at?"

He approached her. "More pleasing with the passage of every day."

Her smile was playful. "Are you sure? Perhaps you should find a second, younger wife?"

He shook his head sadly. "There is only you. Forever."

She came to him, touched his cheek, and went out of the room.

Enki hoped he'd put her at ease. She was all he wanted. Her and the house full of talk, music, and the occasional laughter of Human children.

FOUR

Under a new moon, Enlil walked along the main path of the gardens, heading for the gate the giants were building for Enki. The path threaded through the huts in which the Human lived. He could hear their snoring and coughing, children crying, couples arguing, others crying out in passion. A dog sensed his presence and got to its feet. Before it could open its mouth and begin yapping, he gave it a penetrating look; it circled twice and lay down to sleep.

He saw the partially completed gate in the distance silhouetted against the dim star-lit sky. A few moments later he looked down at the giants sprawled and snoring like beasts in the warm dust next to a jumble of huge, cut blocks of stone. Enlil's nostrils flared in revulsion. He had long ago gotten used to the smell of the Human, but he would never be able to abide the stink of the giants. They were extremely unclean and reveled in their stink like swine.

Enlil picked out Humbaba by the giant's huge unkempt red beard which grew to his knees. One of the other giants farted noisily like a trumpet. Enlil walked out among them and held his staff aloft. With a sound like a buzzing bee, it emitted blinding-white arc light. Humbaba and the others roared in pain as they sat up, holding their hands over their eyes. Humbaba squinted from between his fingers and saw that it was Enlil. He pulled the strap of his dirty fleece garment over his shoulder. "Master, you nearly blind us! What do you want?"

"Come with me," said Enlil.

Humbaba called to his grumbling brothers, "Up with you." The other giants got to their feet. Enlil seemed to float over the fields as he led the giants to a pasture through which a little brook flowed as it left the forest. Enlil stopped and waited for the giants to gather around him.

"I want you to build me a great house here," he said. "I have two wives now and they are beginning to fight. One will live here and the other in my house at Shuruppak."

Humbaba scratched himself under his garment as his brothers waited for him to speak for them. "But Master," Humbaba began, "Lord Enki himself has told us to build the gate for the gardens. We've only just begun and there is much more work to do."

"No matter," said Enlil. "You will work here on my house at night. When the sun rises you can return to your work on Enki's gate. I will give you a hundred days to complete my house."

Enlil walked off and the giants grumbled in anger as they watched his retreating figure. When he was out of sight, Humbaba turned to the others. "Well," he said in a weary voice, "let us take a rest. Whoever wakes first, wake the others and we shall begin." The giants lay down on the grass to sleep.

****

Humbaba and the giants spent the next 39 days putting down a foundation of granite stone blocks for Enlil's house. Finishing that, they lost interest. On the morning of the 40th day, Enlil showed up. Under the light of the new moon, he found the giants sleeping on the ground. He raised his staff, lighting the area brighter than day. Humbaba and the others moaned in pain as they covered their eyes with their hands.

"On your feet!" Enlil commanded.

The giants stood, but kept their backs turned, unable to face the light. Finally, Enlil extinguished his staff. He looked around at the many blocks lying on the ground and the lone, partially completed wall. "Very well," he scowled. "I see that I shall have to oversee your work. Begin now." He sat on a block where he could watch them.

Humbaba motioned to the other giants and they began dragging the huge stone blocks over onto the foundation, notching them into place, one against another. They worked quickly and soon the day drew near. The cool of night dissipated as dim light suffused the sky. The Human on their way to toil in the gardens slowed to watch the giants work. The sun edged over the horizon and began its slow ascent into the sky, increasing the temperature. Humbaba and the other giants had grown tired and were covered in sweat. They continued to work, but slowly and begrudgingly.

"Master," said Humbaba finally, "usually we break fast at this time—and we still have Enki's gate to complete."

Enlil ignored his request as he walked to the corner. "Push in the cornerstone and begin the other wall. Then you can stop."

Humbaba cast an angry look at the other giants. "You heard Lord Enlil." They began pushing the great granite corner stone toward where Enlil stood.

"Quickly, quickly," said Enlil, "I will help you line it up."

Enlil stood between the two blocks as Humbaba and his brother, Barjan, backs bent, pushed against the stone with their shoulders.

"To the left," said Enlil, and the block slid scratchily closer. "More. Push!"

Humbaba grunted and the block slid closer until it was inches from Enlil.

"Almost," said Enlil, "But it's off to the left. Humbaba, push and turn it more."

Barjan stood up. "Master," he said to Enlil, "you should climb up out of there first."

"Quiet. I will line it up first. Humbaba, push!"

Barjan stepped away from the block. Humbaba put his shoulder to the stone and grunting, gave it a mighty shove. The stone slid scratchily several feet along the sand-coated surface. Enlil moaned and was quiet.

Barjan went forward and looked down into the space between the two blocks. "Humbaba," he said, "Enlil is crushed. You have killed a god!"

***

Enki's son Gamilesh and some of his barge crew were visiting. Kish had prepared a feast and Enki and the others were eating and drinking wine when Kish came to tell him that there was a runner outside. "He is greatly agitated," she added.

Enki walked through the garden to the gate and opened it. A Human male excitedly told him that the giant, Humbaba, had accidentally squashed Enlil while they were building Enlil's house.

Enki and the others hurried to the scene. A large group of shouting Human had gathered like a flock of birds. Enki entered the blocked outline of the house and saw Humbaba sitting on a fluted column section, scowling darkly. The other giants talked quietly or sat silently, waiting to see what would happen. Enlil lay motionless on the foundation stones. Enki knelt to examine him. His body was bent unnaturally, an arm broken, the bones splintered like twisted twigs. There was no external bleeding. Enki believed he could be reanimated if he acted quickly. He lifted Enlil, cradling him in his arms, and called over to one of the giants, "What happened here?"

As the giant related the tale, Humbaba began pacing nervously. "It was an accident, Lord," he said, "an accident."

"Very soon," said Enki, "Enlil will tell us whether or not it was an accident."

As Enki carried Enlil's body to his house, he realized the chaos had spread far and wide, now infecting the Anunnaki. He and Gamilesh and the others boarded the transporter for the flight to the temple. Upon landing, Enki left Enlil's body with Gamilesh and the others in the central courtyard.

Enki entered the inner sanctum. He looked up at the Hood of Knowledge where it sat in its cradle. The two red jewels in the serpent eyes that crowned it came to life, glowing in the dimness of the sanctum. During his last command on Sithera, a high priest had raised up an Anunnaki. It could be done.

He took the Hood down and put it on his head. He felt immediate warmth, which slowly became pressure. For minutes or hours, he stood motionless as eons of Anunnaki knowledge and experience filled his consciousness.

With the Hood on his head, he left the inner sanctum. In the courtyard, a large shouting crowd of Human had gathered, surrounding Gamilesh and his crew. Enki approached and they parted to let him through. Enki struggled with the pressure in his head, trying not to stagger.

He knelt and put his hands upon Enlil's cool body. His fingers vibrated as the life force flowed from them into Enlil like an electric current, vibrating molecules, bringing cells to life, releasing endorphins, awakening the body's healing power. A spark of life force left Enki's fingers with an electric snap and Enlil's heart began beating faintly, moving blood to flush his tissues with life-giving oxygen and enzymes.

Enlil groaned in pain and the Human cried out in fear. Enlil sat up and looked about, as if waking from a deep sleep. His features were again the picture of health and he bore no evidence of the horrible disfigurement that he had suffered.

Some of the Human cried in fear and fell to their knees. Others shouted in wonder, "Praise be to Lord Enki, son of Anu!"

Enki returned the Hood to its cradle in the inner sanctum. He would decide Humbaba's fate later together with Enlil and the other Anunnaki. When Humbaba and the other giants heard that Enlil had been raised up, they ran away into the cedar forest. Enlil sent a force of Human soldiers after them, but he himself went back to his pleasure pursuits. Enki returned to the plain and his duties. The Human went back to their work in the gardens and the mines. The piles of gold in the temple chambers grew higher and the chaos began to spread further. Anunnaki now waged war against each other for sport, using Human armies. Enki had flown over one such battle on the plain. Two Human armies hacked each other to death with their bronze swords as their Anunnaki kings sat atop the surrounding hills on their gilded thrones, watching in amusement. And Humbaba and the other giants soon found that they could not survive on their own efforts in the cedar forest and began raiding the fruit trees and stock pens of the gardens and trampling the grain in the fields. Again, and again, Enki attempted to contact the mother ship on the transceiver, but the machine remained cold and quiet.

When Enki thought that the chaos could get no worse, he awoke to find Kish lying cold in death beside him. A terrible sensation filled him, something he had only sensed from a distance before. It was the emotion of loss, he realized, an emotion Anunnaki did not normally have to contend with. He sat on the edge of the bed and looked at Kish's stiff form. In the quiet and darkness of his grief, a thought, like a tiny brightly plumed bird, assailed him. He allowed it to alight. Could he perhaps use the Hood to bring her back to life? "No," he heard himself say aloud. The protocols forbad it, and the chaos was already threatening to overwhelm them.

He wrapped Kish for her death sleep. Afterward he entombed her in his house on the plain and moved his things back up to the Eanna.

***

There was no moon and the stars provided the only light. Dawn would not come for three more hours. The Human slept soundly in their mud and thatch huts as heavy footfalls left the forest and came down the path toward the village. When the large dark figures neared the first hut, the mongrel dog sleeping next to the entryway awoke. Before the startled animal could bark a warning, a huge hand seized it and crushed it like a grape, splattering its remains upon the ground. Inside the hut a Human male thought he heard a rustle on the roof above and sat up in bed. The thatch above him was ripped loudly away and a giant bearded face stared down at him. Before he could reach for his sword, the giant seized him and bit him in half. The female that had been lying beside him screamed and attempted to hide under the bed only to be grabbed and dashed against the dirt floor. Horrified screams came from other huts in the gardens as the giants ate their Human victims alive, smashing the walls of several huts to the ground. After they had slaked their hunger they ran laughing and shrieking back into the forest.

****

High up in a chamber in the Eanna, Enki heard a transporter land on the pad. He opened the door to his quarters. Two of the Human that worked for his son, Nergal, stood at the door. They bowed.

"Lord Enki," said one of them, "one of the ore barges has sunk in the ocean in a storm. Nergal and his family and all the crew have drowned."

For the second time, the awful feeling of loss flooded into Enki's insides like cold seawater, but he kept his face emotionless. "When?"

"Two days past."

Enki said nothing. He was Anunnaki and he must show detachment and strength.

"I am sorry, Lord," said the Human.

Enki looked at him. "I will come to discuss the impact on the scheduling when I am able."

The Human appeared shocked by Enki's words. He bowed, turned and walked away.

The Human soldiers that Enlil had sent out in pursuit of the giants never returned. Enki attempted to enlist the help of Enlil and the other Anunnaki in hunting down the giants in the cedar forest, to no avail. Enlil continued to distract himself with his human females, his sporting wars, and his monument building. The other Anunnaki now living in great houses in the teeming cities on the plain felt no requirement to help.

The giants grew bolder and now rushed out of the forest in daylight to tear animals from their pens and snatch the Human tending their fields. They would then run laughing back into the forest, leaving a trail of torn and bloody clothing behind. Enki continued to entreat the other Anunnaki to help him hunt down and destroy the giants, but his pleas went unanswered and the chaos grew.

Enki, his son Gamilesh and some of his barge crew, and Gamilesh's son, Zeb, waited at the foundation of Enlil's abandoned house. A dozen Human soldiers carrying bronze swords and shields marched in ranks as they approached, their feet raising dust in the dry heat. Enki led the group into the cedar forest. After a while the trail they were following disappeared beneath bushy undergrowth. Above, the tall cedars blocked much of the sunlight and the ferns and smaller trees crowding around their bases absorbed the rest. Here and there bright golden shafts of sunlight punched through the dimness.

Enki scouted ahead and found another faint trail. They followed it for hours, finding no evidence of the giants. They paused to rest and Cerpek, one of the Human barge crew, found a huge spore off the trail behind some rocks. A fresh trail of broken ferns and small trees led off to the north. They followed it to where it ended in a grove of tall, thickly leaved deciduous trees. They searched the area, coming upon a dried-up streambed that lead further up the mountain.

Enki saw that the Human were sweating heavily and falling behind. He held up his hand to signal a stop. "Let us rest here. Then we can follow the streambed to the top to see if we can see anything from above."

The great trees hardly stirred in the quiet. Enki stood with his hand on the hilt of his staff. Gamilesh, Zeb, and the bargemen talked softly. The Human squat on their haunches or sat in the dirt of the trail. Zeb raised his hand to signal that he had heard something in the direction from which they had come. Pulling their swords, he and Gamilesh went back for a look. They returned a few moments later, shaking their heads to indicate they'd found nothing.

Enki and the others fell silent as they stared into the foliage, listening to the occasional soft stirrings of the trees. With a crash, a huge figure burst out of the trees to their left. Enki aimed his staff and the giant thudded to the ground, a smoking hole in his head. A laugh erupted, and another giant lunged out of the foliage on the right. He swung his club with a whoosh of sound, barely missing Gamilesh. Gamilesh swung his sword, cutting the giant on his leg before he ran back into the trees, unfazed. The forest grew silent and still as Enki and the others stared into the foliage. Something fell through the trees overhead making a clipping sound. Enki looked up to see a boulder crashing down through the tree branches. It bounced off the trail with a loud thud and rolled into the underbrush. More boulders, tree trunks, and other debris rained down with the sound of thunder. Enki blasted some of the larger boulders to dust with his staff, but many got through, shaking the ground and rolling about like hail. The barrage stopped suddenly, and Enki heard Zeb wailing. He looked over and saw Gamilesh lying on the forest floor, crushed by a boulder.

Zeb knelt over his father's inert form. While the others made a search of the surrounding forest, Enki went to Zeb and knelt to Gamilesh. His eyes were open in death. Enki pushed them closed.

Zeb turned his tear-stained face to Enki. "Lord, my father is dead!"

As the coldness of loss again filled Enki, he nodded. Saying nothing, he lifted Gamilesh up and carried him as he led the way back to the gardens. After the others had gone, Enki wrapped Gamilesh's body in preparation for interment.

The giants disappeared back into the forest. Enki's escalating losses stunned him, and he delegated his duties, remaining in his house for days upon days.

Footsteps scratched on the stones outside Enki's chambers. He went out. Zeb stood there, his head bowed respectfully. "Lord, I have heard how you raised up the god Enlil. Please...raise up my father!"

"I can not."

"He is your son...please!"

"I can not. It is forbidden."

Zeb turned and went away.

After Enki entombed Gamilesh, he could not sleep for days and he wandered about the Eanna alone. On several occasions, vaporous images of Kish, Nergal and Gamilesh appeared in the stone corridors. Enki would stop and stare until the images faded away. One night he heard a noise outside. He went out into the moonlight and saw a figure in the mists by the tomb of Gamilesh. He went closer. It was no illusion. Zeb was struggling to pry the cover stone off his father's tomb with his sword. He'd managed to move it slightly.

Enki walked up behind him.

Zeb turned in fright. When he saw that it was Enki, his features twisted into anger. "Lord. My father...your own son...grows cold in there. Raise him up!"

"Begone!" Enki growled in anger.

Zeb backed up, scowling. He turned and fled.

The next day Enki used his staff to cut another, heavier, cover stone of dense granite, a hands breadth thick. He used his staff to levitate it and pull it back to the tomb. After he lowered it in place he went into his house.

***

The Blue World years came and spent themselves like waves upon a beach. It was the dry season and the plains were covered with tan-colored grasses. The temperature was high and there was no breeze. Enlil sat on his throne in the dry heat upon a hilltop overlooking all. Drinking wine from a golden, jewel-encrusted cup, he looked out as two Human armies moved slowly toward each other like columns of ants. On one side of Enlil, a male Human attendant held a feathered fan aloft, fanning Enlil slowly. On the other, a pleasing young Human female served grapes and other fruits to Enlil and kept his wine cup filled. Every so often the two Human slaves exchanged surreptitious looks that spoke of their secret love for each other.

Below, the forces of Enlil, led by Zeb, grandson of Enki, wore golden-colored tunics. They trotted toward the forces of Tarsus, who wore tunics of cerulean blue. The shouts and cries of the two armies rose up on the hot air as they drew in sight of each other.

Enlil took a sip of wine. The impending battle quickened his pulse and he noticed again how enticing the female slave's breasts were. Setting his wine cup down, he got up from his throne. "On your knees," he commanded her.

"Lord?" she said, quickly casting a furtive look at her lover who was watching with open-mouthed fear.

"Down," said Enlil.

She knelt on the carpet.

Enlil parted the folds of his skirt and hers and mounted her. She looked up briefly at her Human lover, a tear forming in her eye. Soon Enlil's thrusting caused a change in her and she moaned with pleasure. The male Human began crying with grief, forgetting his fanning. Enlil paused, his face awful in anger, as he looked at the slave. He took one of his hands from her hips and grabbed his staff. "Don't stop!"

The male Human resumed his fanning; Enlil resumed his thrusting; below a trumpet sounded a charge. Enlil finished, depositing his seed with a deep groan. He climbed back up onto his throne, his eyes fixed on the scene below.

Zeb led his troop of gold tunic-clad soldiers in pursuit of ten or so blue tunic-wearing soldiers who ran through a rocky outcrop and into a pasture bounded by large boulders on three sides.

Enlil got to his feet. "No!" he shouted uselessly. "It's a trap. Go back!"

Moments later, Zeb's forces found themselves cut off as rank after rank of blue tunic-clad soldiers swarmed through the opening after them. The Blues shouted with blood lust as they encircled the Golds. Fighting at the head of the Golds, Zeb cut down several Blues before a thrown spear knocked him backward, pinning him to the ground. A loud roar went up as more Blues poured into the pasture. They began hacking the out-numbered Golds to death until the shouts and cries ceased. The battle over, the Blues searched though the bodies, dispatching any they found alive with quick knife slashes across their throats.

High above, Enlil rose from his throne. He threw his cup down in anger, turning the sandy soil dark red.

***

At dawn a pounding came at Enki's door. He dressed and went and opened it. A half dozen or so Human soldiers wearing dirt-encrusted, bloody, gold-colored tunics stood in the dim light. Four of them held aloft the body of his grandson, Zeb, dead upon his shield.

They approached and lay Zeb at Enki's feet. A Human officer knelt on one leg beside the body and looked up at Enki. "Lord. It is said that you can raise the dead. Please, we entreat you. Bring our beloved Commander back to us."

"No," said Enki. As he spoke, he could hear his familiar words as if spoken by someone else. "It is forbidden. Begone!"

The soldiers went away, and Enki picked up his grandson and carried him into his quarters. All day he cut the stones required to make a vault for him, wrapped him for death, and lay him inside.

The next day Ziusudra, Zeb's son, and his family, came to Enki to plead with him to raise up Zeb. Again, Enki refused and sent them away. He had lost almost everything now and was plagued with confusion and pain. This pain—loss—was the everyday lot of the lowly Human, and yet they flourished. He was Anunnaki, a god, and from his earliest beginnings he had known only contemplation, learning, mastery, command, pride, and ka. Now he was struggling to bear up under these new Blue World travails. He barred his door and did not go out of his house.

The Blue World days flew by like wind-blown autumn leaves. Without Enki to enforce order, many Human ran away to hunt and forage in the forest. Grasses, bushes, and trees overgrew the gardens. The mines lay abandoned and quiet. And the jungle reclaimed the temples and the mines of Shuruppak.

One night Enki was awakened by a bright, golden glow flooding through his window. He looked out. In the distance the remaining gold barge burned furiously, sending up a column of sparks into the night sky. They could have destroyed it anywhere, Enki realized, but they had chosen to do it where he would see it. Enki watched angrily, following the rising column of sparks. Slowly his anger morphed into a wish that he was ascending with them, going up and home to Nibiru and his father, Anu.

FIVE

Samyaza took the transporter to the temple complex at the Valley of the Kings. He set it down on a hilltop, starting a small grass fire. He exited and walked through the smoke along the ridge line that led to the temple on the next hill. Passing through the gate, he carefully stepped over the corpses of more than a dozen dead Human, some of them children, lying in the courtyard. He saw Enlil in his chambers in the company of two female Human slaves. Samyaza waited discretely outside until Enlil called him in.

Samyaza bowed slightly. "Brother. You must come to the Eanna at the gardens immediately. Someone broke into the inner sanctum and was attempting to use the Hood of Knowledge to reanimate his Human female in violation of all protocol. Luckily one of our brothers caught him. Come. All your brothers will be there. We must pass judgment."

After exiting the transporter, Enlil and Samyaza walked through the torch-lit passageway of the Eanna, their footsteps reverberating off the stone walls. They entered the Great Hall where the other Anunnaki, some of whom they had not seen in many, many years, were seated on their thrones. Enlil and Samyaza took their seats.

A voice called out to the guards, "Bring in the prisoner."

***

Enki heard the heavy footsteps of the guards as they approached. He knew his brothers would vote to put him to death. And as perverted as that judgment would be, he would welcome it, for perhaps death would put an end to the many sufferings that the Blue World had brought him.

The guards took Enki's Shao cape from him and wrapped him in the plain homespun robes of the Human. They hobbled his legs with chains. Then each guard took one of his arms and they led him into the Hall through a screaming crowd of Human. Enki looked up to see Enlil and Samyaza scowling down at him from their thrones. He looked at his other brothers. Some met his eyes, frowning with disdain, while others looked away. Enki lowered his head. Let death come, he thought, it could be no worse than this.

One of the Anunnaki stood and addressed his brothers. "What Enki has done is egregious. But, more importantly, it is forbidden!" The assembled Anunnaki grumbled in agreement.

"Yes," a strong voice shouted. It was Enlil. "An example must be made of Enki. What he has done is..."

Enki threw back his head and laughed. Astonished silence filled the hall. "Yes," he shouted, "what I have done is against the protocols. And I know how highly you all value the protocols."

The Anunnaki angrily argued among themselves as the Human jeered and shouted at Enki.

Enki's voice rose above the din. "Yes! I am guilty. Do with me what you will. I care not."

Enlil left the Hall and returned a moment later with the Hood of Knowledge in his hands.

The excited Human voices echoing off the stone walls grew louder.

Enlil held the Hood up for all to see and the din subsided. "Enki has committed a crime that would bring a quick sentence of death to any of you." Enlil raised the Hood high over his head. "With this I shall see that he suffers that very fate."

With a roar like thunder, the Human shouted out their approval.

Enlil pulled the Hood on. The chamber quieted as his face darkened, a look of intense concentration coming over him. For several moments nothing happened. Then he began to sweat. Soon the sweat began running down his face. He gasped, evidently in great pain, as all watched in rapt silence. He began walking toward Enki, then paused. Sighing heavily, he almost fell, going down on one knee.

The hiss of worried Human speculation again filled the stone chamber.

Enlil got slowly to his feet and again began moving toward Enki. He raised his staff. "The sentence is death...and I...with the power of the Hood, shall deliver it."

"Death!" the Human began chanting, "Death! Death!"

Enki looked around at their angry, reddened faces. Their eyes were already ripping him to shreds. As Enlil drew closer, the Human voices grew even louder, "Death! Death!"

Enki reacted reflexively, knocking aside the guard next to him. In a rage, the Human rushed forward, engulfing him. He shuffled backward, turned, and swept the Human from his path as others swarmed after him. From behind he felt their hands clawing at his skin. He struck them down right and left as he attempted to fight his way out of the Hall. Taking too long a step, the chain around his ankles caused him to tumble. He fell on top of some Human. Others began pummeling him, his body turning numb from a thousand blows. A strange voice shouted a command. Looking up, Enki watched a Human soldier standing above him slowly raise his sword in a muscled arm. Strangely detached, Enki wondered what death would bring. An endless void? The welcome dissipation of the cold, cursed emotion of loss? Time slowed as the sword began its descent. When it was almost upon him the Human soldier disintegrated in a fiery blast of light and heat.

"Order!" a loud voice was commanding over and over as if from a vast distance. "Order!"

Enki got unsteadily to his feet. He saw several black-clad Anunnaki guards that he did not recognize waving their staffs threateningly as they slowly moved the Human back.

"Order!" the voice commanded again. Enki saw an Anunnaki soldier standing straight and tall not far away. "The mother ship orbits above," the soldier said. "Anu the Great has arrived! His transporter will land at any moment."

The Anunnaki soldier pointed to Enlil. "Take that off!"

Enlil pulled the Hood off and it clattered on the floor. The Human erupted in worried speculation and the soldier raised his hand for silence. The distant roar of a transporter's engine flooded through the stone corridors. Then silence. Moments later footsteps echoed off the stone walls as Anu the Great and his consort entered, followed by their guards. The assembled Anunnaki rose as one from their thrones as Anu took his seat and his consort sat beside him. The assembly again took their seats.

Enlil approached Anu, bowing deeply. "King Anu," he began, "Lord of the Universe...a terrible violation of the protocols has occurred. Enki attempted to use the Hood to raise from the dead..." Enlil turned and pointed to the mob of Human watching with wild, awed faces, "...one of them!"

The Anunnaki and the Human erupted in loud bitter speculation until a solitary anguished voce shouted out, quieting them.

Enki took a few short steps toward Anu and threw himself prostrate onto the stone floor. "Father forgive me. What Enlil says is true. I was going to attempt it. I am sorry."

The hall was completely quiet.

"Stand," said Anu.

As Enki got slowly to his feet, Anu said, "I am already aware of all that has happened."

"We have decided on a sentence of death," said Enlil.

Anu slowly shook his head. "No." He looked over at the guards standing behind Enki. "Release him!"

Enki stepped back as the guards took the chains from his ankles.

Anu looked at him. "You are free."

Enki bowed and moved back.

Anu pointed to the Human, disgust on his face. "Clear them from the chambers!"

The guards quickly herded the Human out of the Hall.

Anu waited for the noise to die down and then he stood and faced the assembled Anunnaki. "At the edge of this solar system there has been a major collision of two smaller worlds. This has had many repercussions and we have been dealing with them. That is why we were not able to arrive at the appointed time. We entered your orbit four days ago. I did not contact you because I wanted to observe."

Anu shook his head somberly. "And I have seen all that I shall ever want to see of your treachery. What you have done here, most of you, violates every protocol I have ever given you.

You have completely corrupted this world and now it is nothing but chaos."

Enki's head hung lower as Anu's words sank in.

"Soon," said Anu, "Meteor 349 will pass within one hundred thousand kilometers of this planet, causing a major crustal shift. Volcanoes around the globe will erupt simultaneously. South will move North; North will move South. The glaciers will melt rapidly, flooding the low-lying areas, including this plain. Your punishment will be to remain here and witness the deaths of your progeny. I have ordered the blasting of a chamber deep into the rock of the Eanna, which shall be your prison. Only Enki will leave this place with me when it is time to return to our world."

Silence prevailed in the hall.

Anu continued, "The mountain passes to the north, west and east will be dammed. When the Human have all been destroyed, all Anunnaki but Enki will enter the chamber to be sealed within. There you shall remain entombed until I return to resurrect you."

No one spoke.

"That is all!" said Anu.

Enki and the others bowed respectfully as Anu and his consort left the hall.

***

As the time drew nigh, Enki could not sleep. He thought of all that had happened and what he had done. Although he had engineered the Human in the image of the Anunnaki, he now believed that the power to do that came not from him, nor from the Hood, but from some unknowable higher power. He had seen a tiny spark of that power in the eyes of the Human. He felt he must do whatever he could to save them, no matter the cost to himself.

One day Enki called Zeb's son, Ziusudra, and his sons and their wives into his chambers.

"There is a great flood coming," he said to them.

Worried speculation ensued. Enki raised his hand for silence. He addressed himself to Ziusudra. "Take all of your people out of the gardens. Go at dawn. I will make sure the sentries do not see you. Walk into the cedar forest for thirteen days toward the setting sun. There you must build a great barge, six hundred paces long and half as wide. And on the barge, you must build a great house. When you have finished, take into the barge the seeds of your wheat and fruits, urns of water and one pair each of all the animals and fowl you use for meat."

***

Soon the rains began. For forty days and nights it came down in almost-solid sheets. The rivers rose over their banks and spread across the plain. The Human began gathering at the bottom of the temple tower. Enki watched them. Other Anunnaki began blasting the great underground chamber that would be their prison until Anu returned for them.

Every day more Human came out of the forests, naked, starving, pleading to be allowed up onto the landing pad stones. The guards drove them off, occasionally killing one or two with their staffs. After a time, Enki could watch no longer and did not come out of the Temple. As he prepared himself to return to the mother ship, he thought of Ziusudra and his children and grandchildren. Would they find safety? He hoped so.

The day of departure arrived, and Enki boarded the transporter with his father and some others and rocketed heavenward. Soon he was in the mother ship and on his way back to his own world. Even though the Anunnaki had long conquered death, Enki knew he would never conquer the loss that would flood his soul whenever he looked up at the night sky and saw the Blue World.

The end